Criminally Scandalous

MM Sports Romance

Criminally Yours

West Greene

Cover Design: Books and Moods

Formatting: Tiff Writes Romance

Editing: Tiff Writes Romance

Proofreading: Kimberly Peterson

For Riley, my reason for everything that I do.

For every person who's ever felt like they'd amount to nothing... this is for you.

Prologue

Pistol

Coach blew his whistle as I stepped into the locker room, drawing everyone's eyes to him. He pointed a finger at me, making me frown, dread swirling in my gut. "Cage, in my office," he ordered before turning on his heel and heading out of the locker room, expecting me to follow him.

"Everything good?" Bryce asked me. He was the closest thing I'd ever had to a friend. He'd taken my brutishness in stride, not even blinking an eye at my angry demeanor. And it had worn me down.

And also made me want him so badly that I ached with my need for him. He was gorgeous with dirty blonde hair and blue eyes. A healthy, golden glow from the sun darkened his skin the slightest bit. He was our star quarterback, and though he'd been getting offers from pro teams since his sophomore year, he stuck college out, determined to get his degree before he went pro so he'd have a Plan B in place. When I'd asked him why, he told me he needed something to fall back on if he suffered an injury that killed his NFL career.

He had so much going for him.

I shrugged at Bryce in answer. I didn't know if everything was good. He frowned at me, but I just turned on my heel and strode after the coach to go see what in the hell he wanted.

"Shut the door," he ordered.

Fuck.

I quietly shut the door and then shoved my hands in the pockets of my jeans as I waited on him to tell me what the hell I'd done now. He steepled his fingers together on his desk and frowned down at some paperwork in front him before bringing his hazel eyes to mine. "Pistol, you're a great player and an amazing asset to the team, but you know that drugs are an automatic disqualification."

"Drugs?" I asked incredulously. I hadn't touched anything—not even weed—since my senior year of high school. "Coach, I haven't touched anything," I promised him.

What the hell was even happening right now?

Coach picked up a piece of paper and silently handed it to me. I grabbed it from him, my eyes widening. Positive for THC.

"What the fuck?!" I exploded. I tossed the paper down and thrust my fingers through my hair. I was panicking. Football was all I had to rely on. I was barely passing my classes—couldn't damn focus. And I was about to lose this, too. "Coach, I swear I didn't—"

He sighed. "I know, Cage. I know." He blew out a soft breath. "But my hands are tied here, son. I have no choice but to boot you off the team."

My entire world was spinning out of control. This couldn't be happening.

"I don't—"

But then, I did. Suddenly, I understood *everything*. I'd stayed at Dad's the weekend before we all got hit with a random drug test. I'd steered clear of him and his friends, but I was broke and was forced to eat the food in his fridge. And considering he slipped weed into any fucking thing he could, I had no doubt I'd ingested some.

"Fuck," I whispered, scrubbing my hands down my face. "I went home the weekend before the drug test," I explained. Sadness clouded Coach's eyes. "My roommate wouldn't pay for me to stay on campus for the holiday break and—"

"I know," he said softly. He stood up and rounded his desk before clapping a hand to my shoulder. "Things will work out, son."

I shook my head. "Football is all I have," I rasped. I already had offers for pro, and now all of that was about to go down the drain. I swallowed thickly. "Coach, I don't have anything else to fall back on."

"You're a smart boy, Cage. You'll figure it out."

I didn't have anything. There was nothing to figure out. I was fucked, and everything I'd done for the past two years to make sure I turned out different... I was now watching all of that hard work swirl down the drain along with my dreams.

Bryce shouted my name as I stormed off the field, heading for the parking lot where my beat-up, rust bucket of a truck was parked at. "Pistol, goddammit, I know you hear me!" he shouted.

I continued ignoring him. It would only be a matter of time before the school hit me with a violation and kicked me out, too. School was over for me. My future was now as bleak as my childhood had been.

"For fuck's sake, Pistol!" Bryce barked, grabbing my shoulder just as I slipped through the gates. I swung around to face him, knocking his hand from my shoulder. I glared at him.

"What?" I snarled. "What the fuck do you want, Bryce?"

"I want you to tell me what the fuck is going on, Pistol. What did Coach want? Why are you leaving? We have practice."

"It's over, Bryce." He frowned at me, concern washing in his eyes. I shoved my hand through my hair before dropping it to my side. "They found THC in my system." Understanding crossed Bryce's face. "It's over for me, Bryce."

"I'm sure if you explain—"

I shook my head. Bryce had the opportunity of meeting my dad once, and those small, few minutes had been enough for him to understand what kind of person he was and what my life had been like before I'd escaped to college.

"Coach said his hands are tied." I blew out a soft breath. "I'll figure my shit out. Don't worry about me."

His frown deepened, and he took a step closer to me, resting his hand on my upper arm. Tingles raced through my body at his touch, and my heart skipped a beat.

"Pistol, I'm always going to worry."

I forced a small smile onto my lips. It was rare I gave them out, and he was the receiver of the majority of them. "I'll be fine," I assured him. "Life has kicked me down enough that I know how to get back up."

He huffed. "Pistol—"

"Cutler, get your ass on the field!" Coach yelled.

I reached up and squeezed his hand before peeling it off my arm. "Team needs you, Cutler. Go on. I'll be in touch." But I knew I was lying.

He stood there for a moment like he was contemplating if he believed me before he finally nodded and raced back onto the field.

We both knew I wouldn't be in touch. Our lives were going in two different directions, and we no longer fit into each other's worlds.

My phone rang on the bench seat beside me. I slowly opened my eyes, staring straight ahead out the windshield into the trees right across from me. I'd been sleeping in my truck for the past two weeks while I applied everywhere I could think to apply for a job. But so far, I hadn't heard anything, and money was extremely tight. I only had three dollars to my name now, and I hadn't eaten in two days because I was trying my best to make them last.

Dread slid through my veins when I glanced down at the random number on my phone. The only time I got random calls like this was if Dad had a new burner. And if he had a new burner, that meant he needed me to do something shady.

But shady meant money in my pocket. I could do one run, right? It would set me up for a little while, at least until I found a job. The runs always paid decently.

With a feeling in my gut that I'd regret this before long, I swiped my thumb across the screen and pulled my phone to my ear. "Yeah?"

"You alone?"

"Yeah," I said again with a tired sigh. "What is it?"

"Need you to do a run. I know you didn't want to do this anymore, but Ross got arrested on his last run. I need someone I can trust on this."

A bad feeling slid through my gut, but I ignored it. Just because Ross got caught didn't mean I would. I'd done this so many times, I'd lost count. I knew the best routes to take, no matter where I had to go.

"Where am I picking up at?"

I got the information I needed and shifted my truck into drive on the promise he'd have gas money for me, and he'd just take it out my portion of the money when I got back. I tightened my fingers on the steering wheel, wishing the bad feeling in my gut would disappear.

Sirens lit up the night right before the red and blue lights began flashing in my rearview mirror, lighting up the interior of my truck. I cursed, my heart racing in my chest. I slowly pulled to the side of the road, my heart in my throat.

I was fucked. No goddamn doubt about it.

"Step out of the truck with your hands above your head," an officer ordered, a gun trained on me.

Sweat beaded along the collar of my shirt. I shoved the door open before putting my hands on my head and slowly sliding out of the truck. Two other officers jumped into the back of my truck, revealing the bars of coke hidden there. I squeezed my eyes shut, nausea swirling in my gut.

My life was fucking over. In the span of two weeks, I'd managed to fuck my entire life up.

"Lay flat on the ground with your hands behind your back," the officer ordered, his gun still trained on me. Silently, I did as he said. As soon as he began to cuff me, he began reading me my Miranda rights. I kept my mouth shut all the way to the station until I was given my single phone call.

But Dad never answered.

Chapter One

Bryce

I slowed to a walk as I came up on my house. I'd seen the mailman go by, so I knew my mail had already been delivered—if I had any. I went basically paperless on everything. Usually, all I got was random sales papers that I never bothered to look at. I usually just gave them to my neighbor, Mrs. Thomson, since she loved couponing. Besides, it was something small to brighten a woman's day, and Mrs. Thomson always looked out for me anyway.

In fact, during the football season—which was coming up a lot sooner than I wanted it to—she kept an eye on my house and even cleaned it for me. I made a shit ton of money being the starting quarterback for the Patriots, but I hated letting strangers mess with anything of mine.

That and I was raised humbly. I invested a lot of my money and donated to a lot of charities. I tried to do what I could to help other people out.

Besides, I couldn't take all that money with me when I died. The hell was I going to do with it all?

I lived in a small, two-story house in a cul-de-sac. Most of the people in the neighborhood were elderly. I usually helped Mr. Johnson two houses up rake his leaves every fall, and Mrs. Orson always needed help weeding her garden in the summer. It had taken the tight-knit community a moment to warm up to me, but when they did, they welcomed me with open arms.

They really were some of the nicest people I'd ever met. And even better? They didn't give two shits about my pro-footballer status. Don't get me wrong—the men watched football, but they didn't have freakouts over me. In fact, most of them hated the Patriots, so I got more shit than anything. But I loved it.

Here, I was just another regular person.

I waved at Mr. Ingle across the street. He was sitting in his rocking chair, probably working on his fourth cup of coffee of the day. He waved back, and then I turned and grabbed my mail. I paused in my driveway when a letter from the federal prison back home caught my eye.

What the fuck?

I quickly walked into my house and set the other mail on the counter before peeling the flap open and taking out the letter.

Bryce,

I don't even know if you're going to remember me, to be honest. It's Pistol. I guess you probably got that from the envelope, though. If you don't remember me, I can't really blame you. I mean, we weren't exactly best friends, but you were the only person who saw past the poor kid on a scholarship and saw me—just a guy trying to better his life.

The school expelled me when my drug test came back negative—literally got expelled the day after I got kicked off the team. I lived in my truck for a couple of weeks applying for jobs. I didn't want to go home—place was absolute shit. You met my dad once, so I'm sure you get it if you remember him.

But I only had three dollars to my name then, and when he called, I stupidly answered. And despite the bad feeling in my gut, I agreed to do what he asked me.

And I got caught—like a

fucking dumbass.

I've been in prison for six years now. Shit's rough, but I'm making it. Someone managed to get your address for me. I've had it for a few months now but only just got the courage to write you. I'm not even sure if you'll read this far. I mean, what successful guy wants to have anything to do with a convict, right?

I'm supposed to be getting out soon. My next hearing is in a couple of weeks, and I'll find out then if I make parole. I—

Fuck, I got interrupted and forgot what I was going to write. Shit, I hate when that happens. Fucker can't get a damn moment of peace in this shithole, I tell you.

But it's time to eat. I guess I'll mail this out. If I don't ever hear from you, I'll understand. To be honest, I wouldn't want to hear from me either.

Pistol.

Fuck.

Holy shit.

Pistol was in *prison.*

I scrubbed a hand down my face and leaned heavily against my counter, staring down at his letter. I'd never forgotten about him. I had tried calling him and finding him, but I never wanted to invade his privacy by hiring a personal investigator. Instead, I finally got the memo and figured he wanted to cut ties with me. So, I let him go.

Instead, he'd been stripped bare of his rights and tossed into prison.

My heart ached for him. It physically hurt me to know he was locked behind bars. He had already been trapped, trying to escape his father's clutches in college, and now, he was trapped even more.

He'd mentioned parole in his letter. Where in the hell would he even go if he got out? Back to his dad's?

I snorted. Yeah—no. Like fuck was I allowing that to happen. Could I possibly pull strings and get him here in Massachusetts? I didn't know much about the judicial system, but there had to be *something* I could do to help him, right?

Frowning, I pulled my phone out of my pocket and called my attorney. He answered on the third ring. "Not often you call me, Cutler. Should I be worried?"

"I don't think so. At least, not yet." He sighed. I knew he had another player he was an attorney for that constantly kept him on his toes. I really didn't want to add to his troubles, but I needed to help Pistol any way I could. He'd already suffered enough. "I have a friend from college who might be getting parole soon. He has a hearing in a couple of weeks. Do judges sometimes grant people to move out of state?"

"Under special circumstances," Jackson

said. "Are you trying to move this friend in with you?"

"Um, well, yeah," I said, shrugging. "I'm all he's got, and I don't think him getting out and being back in the same place he was before will help him at all."

Jackson sighed, and I could picture him in my mind's eye rubbing his forehead as he thought over what I was suggesting. "Christ. Do you know if this friend of yours has an attorney?"

"No," I muttered. "I, um, just heard from him for the first time today. It's a bit... complicated."

"Kid, when someone's in prison, it's never *not* complicated. Give me the guy's name, and I'll do some digging, find his attorney, and see if something can't get figured out. Just know you might have to show up at his hearing."

"I'll do whatever it takes," I assured Jackson. "Thank you. I'll send you a bonus."

He chuckled. "Anyone ever told you that you're too nice for your own damn good, Jackson?"

I sheepishly shrugged a shoulder, my cheeks burning a little red. “Well, it’s just—”

“I know, kid. I was teasing you. Don’t change, yeah? And I’ll keep you up to date.”

I grinned. “His name is Pistol Cage, and he’s in Washington County State Prison.”

“What a fucking name,” Jackson muttered. “Alright. Ill be in touch.”

Pistol,

Fuck, man, I am so glad to hear from you. I tried calling you so many times, but I eventually just figured you were trying to cut ties with me. I wish you'd reached out sooner.

I'm sorry you felt like you had to turn to him for help. If you'd just come to me, Pistol, you could've just crashed with me until you got things figured out. I'd have hidden you from the administrators. We would've figured it out. I've always been in your corner, and that hasn't changed.

Please don't be angry with me for sticking my nose where it doesn't belong, but I contacted my attorney, and we're going to try to set you up here with me in Massachusetts if you get out on parole in a couple of weeks. I want to help you, and I'm hoping you'll let me this time. You don't have to return to whatever you came from. I can help you get on your feet, Pistol.

If your attorney talks to you about this, please be open. I'm begging you. I've always considered you a close friend.

I've got my fingers crossed that you get parole in the coming *weeks. I'll do my best to arrange a visit before then though. I'd like the opportunity to see you again, if that's okay with you.*

I look forward to hearing from you.

Your friend,

Bryce

With a sigh, I folded up the letter before sliding it into an envelope. Then, I cringed when I realized I didn't have stamps. Hell, it was a miracle I had envelopes and a yellow notepad stashed in my office. I didn't even remember why I bought them.

I glanced at the sales papers on the counter where I'd left them and snatched them up, hoping Mrs. Thomson would have a stamp I could use. I'd get some from the post office tomorrow and give her three to make up for the one I borrowed.

She answered her door with a wide

smile on her face. "Bryce! Come in. I just made some cookies. Do you want one? You're not on that strict diet yet, are you?"

I laughed softly, setting her sales papers where I normally did on her living room table before following her into the kitchen. "No, ma'am, I'm not, thank God. Football wouldn't be half as bad if I could just eat what I want."

She laughed and handed me a fresh, gooey, soft chocolate chip cookie. I moaned in delight, closing my eyes to better savor the burst of sugar on my tongue. "What's that in your hand, hun?"

I glanced down, and a light blush skittered across my cheeks. "I, um, well, it's a long story. Can I borrow a stamp though?"

She laughed and opened her kitchen drawer of miscellaneous crap before ripping one off her book and handing it to me. I quickly peeled it off and slapped it on the corner of the envelope. She closed her drawer back and handed me another cookie. "Now, tell me this long story."

My blush deepened. "I, um, it's a guy I had a crush on in college. He got into some trouble, and I didn't know it, but he finally reached out to me, and well, I'm trying to help him."

She rolled her eyes at me. "That's not such a long story, Bryce."

"Well, he's in prison," I sheepishly admitted.

She patted my arm, handing me yet another cookie when I polished off the second. She loved feeding me sweets during my off-seasons. "Hun, if you like him enough to still blush like a boy in puberty, then he's obviously a decent guy. What's your plan?"

I relaxed a little. "Well, if I can make it work, I'll move him up here with me if he's able to get parole. I'll help him get his life together."

She wiggled her eyebrows at me. "And maybe attempt to defy science and make babies while your at it?"

I almost dropped the cookie. "Mrs. Thomson!"

She bent over a little, laughing so hard she was wheezing. "I love messing with you, kid. Come on. Let's go sit on the porch and see if we can't get Mr. Ingle to come on over and sit with us, too."

"Still crushing on him?" I teased. Mrs. Thomson lost her husband seven years ago, and though she said she'd never move on from her late husband, she was still determined to flirt while she still had it. Her words—not mine.

She winked at me. "At least I can own up to it, boy."

My cheeks reddened all over again. Sometimes, I really hated that I blushed so damn easily.

Chapter Two

Pistol

I couldn't believe he actually wrote me back. I was...astounded, to say the least. Shocked. A little confused.

He'd tried to reach out to me.

My heart thudded hard in my chest. Bryce Cutler, the guy who had everything, had never forgotten about me, and in a heartbeat, he'd reached out to me again as soon as he had the chance. And now, he was bending over backward to try to help me.

I didn't deserve his help. I really didn't. And it made me a little uncomfortable.

But I couldn't ignore the surge of happiness I felt, too. Finally, someone was in my corner. I'd been alone in this hell hole for six goddamn years. When I got here and was allowed to have my one phone call, Dad had never answered the phone. I guess I shouldn't have expected him, too. He never gave a damn when any of his other men took the fall for one of these runs.

But I was his *son*. I really thought he would have cared at least a little bit.

But he hadn't.

So, when he showed up on one of my visitation days five years ago, I told him to fuck off and to never contact me again. I was done with him and his shit. I was done with the drugs. Done with all of it. And before Bryce, I had no idea what the hell I was going to do when I got out of here, but I knew I would *never* go back to him, that house, or that fucking town.

I'd sleep under a bridge somewhere and starve before I ever trusted that fucker of a man again.

But Bryce was trying to get me help. He

was trying to get me out of this state. He was going to let me live with him.

I'd read his letter five times already, thinking maybe all my time inside and all my loneliness made me imagine his words—hallucinate them—but nope. They were there in black and yellow in his neat scrawl that made my own handwriting look like pure chicken scratch.

Bryce had *never* given up on me, and even now, he wasn't.

All those feelings I thought I'd finally done away with came roaring back, clenching my chest, pulsing through my veins.

I was still head over heels, madly in love with the starting quarterback for the Patriots.

I was well and truly fucked. But despite my thoroughly fucked status—and not in the way I wanted to be—I still decided to write him back.

What could I say? I just seemed to be a glutton for punishment.

Bryce,

Would you believe me if I said I had to reread your letter multiple times to believe the words you wrote? I've been on my own in here for so long that the thought of someone finally giving a damn... well, I didn't really believe it.

If what you have planned works out, I don't know how I'll ever repay you. I'll owe you my life, really. Because if this works out, you'll be saving mine. I've got nothing outside of this jail cell. I want out so badly, and at the same time, just as much, I'm terrified to leave. Because I know there's no meals, no warmth, no comfort once I get out of here if I can't figure something out and fast.

I'd love for you to come visit me. The next visitation day is Wednesday. I'm not sure if you can make it, but if you can, I'd love the opportunity to see you face-to-face again.

Anyway, there's not much happening here on my end. Life is just the same old thing, day in and day out. I eat, get stuck in my cell, eat again, maybe get a chance to go out in the yard, eat, shower, and then it's lights out.

I'd love to hear what's going on out there in the real world though, and I still love football as much as I did when I was enrolled in school, so if you want to talk football, I'm all ears…or well, eyes, really, I guess.

I hope to hear from you again,

Pistol

* * *

Bryce

My feet pounded the concrete as I pushed myself to close the last bit of remaining distance between me and my house. I'd already seen the mailman go past me, which meant if I had any mail, it would be waiting in my mailbox for me. I'd been obsessively checking since I sent my letter to Pistol, and with each day that passed, I was becoming more and more fearful that I'd overstepped, and he was shutting off communication between us.

I slowed to a jog and then finally came to a stop in front of my mailbox. I flung open the door, hope curling in my chest when I saw the small envelope sitting there. I quickly snatched it out, my stomach flip-flopping when I saw it was from Pistol.

Not even bothering to go inside the house to read away from the prying eyes of my neighbors, I sat on the porch steps and ripped open the envelope, reading through his words, my anxiety easing with each word I read.

But in place of that anxiety, worry and sadness for him crept in its place. Pistol was having a hard time of it, and I hated it. I hated that he was in that position. And I hated even more that his father had ever put him in that kind of position. And even more than that, I wished Pistol had realized back then that I would have done anything to help him.

Instead, for six years now, he'd been stuck in prison with no one to support him.

"Hey, hun," Mrs. Thomson said, surprising me. I jerked my head up. She was coming up my drive, holding a tray of cookies. With a huff, she lowered her aging body down onto the step next to me and offered me a cookie. "Is that a letter from my future son-in-law?"

I chuckled. Mrs. Thomson said I was basically her son, and honestly, I loved it. I loved that I had my own little family of sorts away from home. And when my parents came to visit me during my off-season, my mom and Mrs. Thomson always spent time together, doing so much shopping that I had to ship everything to my parents' house down south so they didn't pay obscene baggage fees on the planes.

"Yeah. I feel like I've been waiting on pins and needles for him to finally write me back. Letter writing sucks."

She barked out a laugh. I snagged a cookie, groaning at the chocolatey goodness when it just seemed to melt in my mouth. "You'd have hated living back in my day then, Bryce. Letter writing was our thing, especially when my husband was away at war. There were no phone calls or text messages."

I faked a grimace that had her laughing. "Sounds like a nightmare."

She lightly smacked me. "You kids have no idea how easy you have it with phones that you can carry around with you everywhere, computers, internet that just floats through the air—"

I laughed so hard I thought I was going to break a rib. She huffed, smacking me again. I rubbed my arm, surprised at her strength, but I still couldn't stop laughing. "Internet floating through the air?" I snorted.

"See if I ever bring you cookies again for laughing at me," Mrs. Thomson snipped.

I leaned over and kissed her cheek. "You'd never deny me of these during my off-season," I teased her.

She just cut me a side-eye. I bit back my grin. "Okay—okay, I'm sorry. But just so you know, internet doesn't just float through the air. There are satellites and—"

"Boy, I am not stupid. I was just trying to distract you," she informed me.

I grinned at her. "Well, it worked." I looked back at Pistol's letter. "He's having such a hard time, Mrs. Thomson. I just want to wrap him up in my arms and never let go."

She handed me another cookie, and when I grabbed it from her, she rubbed my back. "When he gets out in a couple of weeks—because he *will* get out, hun—you'll make everything all better for him. I know you will."

A tight smile pulled at my lips. I really hoped I could help him, make things better for him. He deserved a chance to just rest, but knowing Pistol, he would be trying to get on his feet as soon as possible and wouldn't take some time to just be and enjoy his freedom—or, well, at least as much freedom someone could get while on parole.

"He wants me to come visit him," I told Mrs. Thomson. "I think I'm going to." I looked over at her. "Want to fly with me and keep me company?"

She beamed at me. "You mean you want to travel with this old lady?" she teased.

I laughed, taking another cookie. "Mrs. Thomson, you're not old." She rolled her eyes at me. "And yes, I want you to travel with me. You'll have to find something to do while I'm visiting him, but I'd love to have your company."

She patted my hand. "Then I guess I better start packing, huh? When are we leaving?"

I sheepishly smiled at her. "Tomorrow?"

She laughed and stood with a grunt. "Tomorrow it is then, Bryce." She ruffled my hair before heading down my porch. I watched her until she disappeared behind her front door. Then, I got up and headed inside the house to write a simple letter to Pistol.

No sense in writing something lengthy when I could say everything I wanted to when I finally got to visit him.

Pistol,

I'll be seeing you Wednesday.

Bryce

With that, I folded the piece of paper, slipped it into an envelope, and then headed to the post office to see if I could rush ship this letter. I wasn't all that familiar with rush shipping things, but for Pistol, I'd try. Because I wanted him to know he had company this Wednesday.

He wasn't alone anymore. Never again.

I wasn't letting him suffer and fight by himself anymore.

From here on out, it would be us against the world, and no matter what, Pistol would *always* have me standing in his corner.

Chapter Three

Pistol

"Cage, let's go. You've got a visitor."

I looked up in surprise before getting up from my cot, following the guard out of the cell and toward the visitation area. I'd gotten Bryce's letter the very next day after it was postmarked, letting me know he was coming to see me, though I hadn't really allowed myself to believe it. I mean, could I have really expected someone as wealthy and successful as Bryce to make time for a criminal like me?

Nah, not really, when you really

thought about it. It just didn't mesh—*we* didn't mesh.

The room I was led into was a bit crowded. Circular tables were placed seemingly randomly throughout the room, and multiple people were sitting at the tables, the ones in jumpsuits on one side, and their visitors on the other.

I scanned the room as I was moved through the tables to an empty one, and once I was sitting, the guard moved to the wall closest to me, no doubt to keep an eye on me. I mean, fuck, this was the first visitor I'd had in the entire six damn years I'd been locked up in this hell hole. I'd be wary too if I was him.

The door on the other side buzzed before it opened. A prison guard strode in, and then a tall, muscular guy walked in behind him wearing jeans and a plain black t-shirt. I swallowed thickly, that blonde hair and those hazel eyes as familiar to me as my own reflection.

Bryce had come. He'd *actually* come to see me.

My heart raced in my chest, and my

palms began to sweat. He was here. He was actually fucking here.

It was a bit hard for me to believe, even if he was making his way over to me with a slight smile tilting his lips. He didn't even look nervous, but then again, why would he have a reason to? It wasn't like he was madly in love with me—not like I was with him. He didn't have any reason to be nervous.

Bryce took a seat at the table and laced his fingers together on top, leaning forward a little. He ran his eyes over me, studying me, taking me in. It was making me nervous, but I was pretty fucking proud of myself for not fidgeting. I'd thankfully gotten out of that habit a few years ago. You quickly learned to recognize and stop your nervous quirks in a place like this. People in prison could sniff out fear and nerves like hungry wolves.

"Hey," he finally breathed, breaking the tension hanging between us. I relaxed a little—well, as much as I could. I hadn't let my guard down in six years. "You've... changed," he settled on.

I shrugged. "Place like this will do that to you."

A frown tugged at his lips as he nodded. "Yeah, I guess it would." He blew out a harsh breath. "I wish you would've reached out a hell of a lot sooner than you did, Pistol. You wouldn't have been alone all these years."

I shrugged. Alone was what I was used to. Being alone was the only thing I could rely on. It was the one thing I knew would never let me down.

And I was terrified as fuck of Bryce one day letting me down. I wasn't sure if I could ever recover from it, to be honest.

"You get used to doing things on your own eventually."

Bryce shook his head. "Shouldn't have to when people are willing to be in your corner." He shoved his fingers through his hair, staring down at the table. "It's killing me to know that you've been in here all this time with no one to visit you, making you feel like nobody gave a fuck." He raised those hazel eyes to mine, sucking me into their depths. God, I could *drown* in them and die happily. "I give a fuck, Pistol. I've *always* given a fuck."

I clenched my hands together in my lap, my heart in my throat. "I wasn't sure if you'd care to hear my story once you found out I was arrested," I said quietly.

He reached across the table and then growled low in his throat when he remembered he couldn't touch me. My eyes tracked the movement of his hand as he snatched it back, my skin tingling at the mere *thought* of him touching me. I wanted his skin on mine so bad.

Bryce shook his head, shoving his hand through his hair again in agitation, but I knew it wasn't toward me. It was toward the situation we were in, the fact that he couldn't be as open with me as he wanted. Fuck, it was driving me nuts, too.

"Pistol, you'd have to do something really fucking stupid for me to ever turn my back on you. I'm talking about something you can't come back from. What you did?" He shook his head. "It just makes me want to hunt your dad down and make him pay for every moment you've suffered and for turning his back on you when you needed him the most."

A lump formed in my throat. Bryce really did care, and the fierceness of his protectiveness of me seemed to have only gotten stronger over time.

My heart warmed, my soul relaxing in his presence. I wasn't alone, and despite my fears, I knew Bryce wouldn't abandon me, wouldn't turn his back on me. He was here to stay.

I offered up a small smile, wishing I could reach forward to touch him, too. But that would just get me beaten with one of the prison guard's batons, and I wasn't keen on that happening. I wouldn't do *anything* to jeopardize me possibly getting parole.

"I'm really glad you came," I said quietly, sincerity ringing in my voice.

He cracked a grin, and I just about melted in my seat. God, why did I have to be so in love with him?

"I'm glad I came, too, Pistol."

Bryce

I sipped at my coffee, gently rocking back and forth on the rocking chair on my porch. Two days ago, Ms. Thomson said I needed rocking chairs if I expected her to come over to visit, so I'd gone out and purchased two white ones, sticking them on my porch, and then I'd gone out and bought a small table to position between them.

She was right though. Rocking chairs made all the difference. Now, after my run every morning, I came out here with my cup of coffee and enjoyed watching the neighborhood slowly wake up.

I glanced down at the letter in my lap, a bit scared to open it. Pistol said he would write me again when he found out anything about his parole hearing, and I knew this letter would contain information on it.

Blowing out a soft breath, I set my coffee aside and then slowly ripped the envelope open before grabbing the folded piece of paper out.

Bryce,

My parole hearing is in two days. I'm hoping this makes it to you fast enough, but just in case it doesn't, if I get out, they'll give me a phone call, so I'll be able to call the number my attorney gave me to get in touch with you.

The hearing is on the 4th at 10:15.

I'm super fucking nervous for it, Bryce. I feel sick to my stomach just thinking about it. All of the what-ifs are freaking me the fuck out.

Don't bother writing me back until after the hearing. Because if I get out, I'm not sure if I'll ever receive the letter.

Pistol.

Yeah, fuck that. I was writing him, and I would make sure it made it to him before his hearing. I couldn't let him sit with all of this anxiety without reminding him I was standing in his corner. I was nervous as hell for his hearing, too, but we'd get through this.

Together.

Just like I promised.

Standing, I headed into the house. Setting my coffee cup on the desk in my office, I sat down and grabbed the yellow notepad and snatched up my pen, getting ready to write him back.

Pistol,

Yeah, you should've known I wasn't going to listen. Like fuck am I sitting here, letting you freak out like that. It's nerve-wracking as hell for both of us, but we'll get through this. We'll get through it TOGETHER like I promised. I'll always remain in your corner, Pistol.

I'll be there for your hearing. Don't ever doubt that. And if you get out, I'll be there waiting for you, and I'm not coming back home until you're on the plane with me, you hear? I've got a real good feeling in my gut that if you get out, they'll grant you permission to come live with me.

I'll see you in two days. Hang in there.

Bryce

I neatly folded the letter and then stuffed it into an envelope before heading out to the post office to do what I did the last time I needed him to get a letter fast. I didn't care how many letters I had to expedite. If he remained locked up, I'd just get used to frequent visits down south and expedited letters.

Fuck, I was whipped. But I guess I always had been. Pistol meant the world to me, and I wasn't letting him slip through my fingers again.

And my first step to doing that was making sure he realized I would be a permanent fixture in his life. Pistol Cage wasn't getting rid of me. Not this time.

Chapter Four

Bryce

I had very little time to get together everything I needed for Pistol. I had three bedrooms, but only two were furnished–mine and the guest room. And I didn't want to change the guest room into Pistol's room. Which meant I used some of the money I just had sitting aside to purchase an entire new bedroom set. Then, I purchased a gray and black bed set. I even put a black rug by the bed.

Ms. Thomson laughed at me when I dragged her shopping with me to get things for his bathroom, hangers for his closet, and other small decorations to make his room really feel like his.

I probably went overboard, but I was excited. And I wanted Pistol to be comfortable and feel at home. Most of all, I wanted to him have a space in my house that was all his, a space that could be his safe place when he felt overwhelmed and needed some time to breathe and get himself back together.

I knew there was a possibility he might not be granted parole, and my attorney hadn't heard for sure if he would even get to come up here if parole was granted, but I wanted to set it up anyway. Because *if* he did get out and got to come up here, I wanted everything to be ready.

"You did an amazing job," Ms. Thomson told me as we sat at my table eating cookies.

I shrugged. "I just want him to be happy and comfortable here," I told her.

She patted my hand. "It's a lot more than that, hun, and you can't convince me otherwise. You never stopped loving that boy." She patted my hand one more time before she grabbed another cookie from the tray. "You'll be good for him. I know you will."

I sighed and sank my teeth into the chocolatey goodness. I only hoped she was right.

* * *

I'd never been to court before, so I wasn't sure what to expect. All I'd ever seen were the court shows my dad watched on TV, and I hadn't ever figured out if those were realistic expectations or not.

What I stepped into was quite different. Probably the biggest difference between civil and criminal court cases.

A line of about five men in jumpsuits was led into the room, shackled and cuffed together. The officers with them were armed. They all sat in the very front row behind the small table.

I instantly recognized Pistol. He was between a skinnier guy and another guy about half his size. Pistol was easily the biggest man sitting there, and something hot surged in my veins at the sight of his broad shoulders.

Fuck, I had it bad for him.

"All rise," an officer announced. I quickly stood to my feet. The doors to the right of the stand opened, revealing the judge. She was wearing a black robe. Her skin glistened under the lights, and she moved with power and grace, her steps unhurried. Once she was seated, the officer called out, "You may be seated."

I took my seat again, waiting on bated breath for Pistol's turn to come up. Both men before him were denied their parole, and my stomach twisted in knots. What if she denied Pistol's, too? I wasn't sure if I could handle it. It would hurt me, but it would destroy every bit of hope Pistol had.

"Pistol Cage." She shook her head with a small laugh. "Can I ask who the hell named you?" she asked, looking at Pistol.

He shrugged. "I think my mother did, your honor, but I never got the opportunity to ask."

She hummed and linked her fingers together, looking him over. "You have no priors, and you've kept yourself clean and out of trouble the entire time you've been locked up. First, I want to say well done. I know it's hard to stay out of trouble and keep to yourself in there, and you did it. You should be proud of that. As your judge, I am proud of you."

I swallowed thickly. She hadn't said *anything* like this to the two men before him.

"Because of your exceptional behavior, I will grant your parole. And after your first two years of parole, we'll see about shortening it." I relaxed. He was, at the very least, getting out today. "I am also going to grant your move to Massachusetts to live with Bryce Cutler. I believe a clean break will do you even better."

I could've kissed that woman, I was so fucking happy.

"You'll check in with your parole officer once a week, clear? And I expect you to get your butt back down here once a month for a drug and alcohol screening and a wellness check. Is that understood?"

"Yes, your honor." I couldn't mistake

the shaking in his voice. He was emotional. Fuck, who could blame him? He was fucking getting out today.

And he was coming home with me.

I watched as Pistol's shoulders sagged in relief, and he turned his head a little, shooting me a small smile. I grinned at him.

I was finally getting him out of this hell hole.

Pistol rolled his shoulders as he walked out of the gate. I straightened up from my leaning position on my car and grinned as he got closer. He'd put on a lot of bulk in prison. He'd been a tall, stocky guy in college, but now, there wasn't an ounce of fat on his body—everything pure, hard muscle. Fuck, he looked hot as sin.

"Hey," he gruffly greeted. He shoved his hands in his pockets. "I don't have anything with me."

Hell, his clothes barely fit him. I tapped the roof of the car. "Come on. Get in. We'll go grab you some clothes."

He swallowed thickly. "You sure about this, Bryce? I can't pay you back. Not anytime soon, anyway."

I opened my car door. "I don't want payment, Pistol. I just want to help you get on your feet."

With that, I slid into the car. He continued standing there for a moment and then finally got in as well. First stop, a clothing store to get him some clothes that fit until I could take him shopping back home. Then, we would grab dinner before I returned the car and we hit the airport.

"This yours?" he asked me. "It's clean as hell."

I snorted. "No, not mine. I rented it. I've got clearance for you to fly, and just a note before I forget, you'll need to get clearance every time you fly back here to meet with your parole officer."

He grimaced. "I don't have money for plane tickets."

"Pistol," he glanced at me, "I never mentioned you needing to find money. I just said you'll need to get clearance. I'll take care of everything. Don't worry about it."

He did look bothered by it though; he just didn't voice more of his concerns. Sighing, I relaxed in my seat as much as I could. I knew this would be an adjustment for him, but hopefully, I could get him on board before long.

Pistol was obviously hungry as fuck. When I told him for the third time not to worry about the price of what he was ordering, he finally ordered himself a steak with potatoes and greens. I ordered an appetizer of fried mushrooms, which he mostly devoured by himself.

I didn't mind, and I didn't say a damn word about it. I was just glad he was finally relaxing around me. His hunger probably won out over his pride though.

"I wanted to talk to you about something," I told him once I was done chewing my piece of broccoli.

He grunted, glancing up at me. "Talks never go well."

I remembered that all too well. The last talk he'd had with someone while he was free ended with him being kicked off the football team and eventually out of school.

"It's nothing bad—well, not to me, I guess. Depends on how you take it."

He grunted again, shoving a piece of steak into his mouth. I scratched at my chin, hating the stubble that was growing in already. Fuck, I needed to shave. I hated having prickly skin.

"I'm constantly in the media, and someone will get wind before long that I have you living with me. They're going to dig into your past and blast it all over the news. Are you okay with that? If not, I can rent a house for you—no problem."

He shook his head. "I stopped giving a fuck what people say about me a long time ago, Bryce. Worrying about what other people think gets me nowhere. So I really don't give two shits."

I snorted. "Still just as crass, huh?" I teased.

Finally, a small smile tilted his lips. He shrugged. “Keeps the losers away.”

I barked out a laugh. “You’ll fit right in with my neighbor, Ms. Thomson. She’s excited to meet you, by the way.” I was rambling now, but I didn’t care. He was listening, and that was all that mattered to me. “I live in a community of older people. It’s quiet and nothing happens there. And I’m sort of friends with them all, though Ms. Thomson is pretty special to me. She likes to bake me cookies every single day during my off seasons.”

Pistol snorted. “She sounds like a character.”

I grinned. “You’ll love her; I just know it. And the two of you will get along great.”

He hummed. “If you say so, Bryce.”

I just rolled my eyes at him. He didn’t give himself enough credit. Ms. Thomson would love him, and I knew she would, even if it was solely for the reason that he made me so damn happy.

Chapter Five

Pistol

I wasn't sure what I was expecting when we finally got to Pistol's house in the middle of the night, but I definitely was *not* expecting him to have gone all out of his way to set me up my own bedroom, complete in dark tones with that brand new furniture smell.

"I'm sorry I don't have clothes for you. I wasn't sure what size you wore—"

"Bryce," I said quietly, my voice thick with emotion I couldn't hide, "this is perfect. Amazing. Thank you. I never expected anything like this when you offered for me to come live with you."

He rubbed the back of his neck with a sheepish smile. Then, he shrugged. "Well, I was a bit excited," he explained. "I didn't overstep, did I?"

I chuckled and toed off my shoes, shaking my head. "I've got no complaints as long as you or your bank account doesn't," I assured him. In the very short time I'd been out of prison so far, I'd figured out Bryce liked to take care of people. Since I'd figured that out at the restaurant we'd eaten at before heading to the airport, I'd just kept my mouth shut whenever he did something for me.

Sure, I'd say something if he started doing too much, but caring for others was his love language.

Love.

Fuck, I needed to get my head on straight. And I obviously needed some fucking sleep.

There was no way Bryce felt the same way about me.

"I'll be up in a couple of hours for my morning run, and I've got practice a few hours after that. If you're up, I'll introduce you to Ms. Thomson before I leave."

I nodded and sank onto the edge of the bed, a small groan leaving my lips when I realized the mattress was super fucking soft. God, I'd *never* had a bed this soft. Bryce was spoiling the shit out of me.

"Sounds good."

Bryce smiled at me and backed toward the door. "If you need anything, I'm just down the hall," he said, throwing his thumb over his shoulder. "I'll, um, probably see you in the morning. Sleep well."

He slipped out of the room, quietly shutting my bedroom door behind him with a soft click. I blew out a soft breath and flopped back on the mattress with a groan, scrubbing my hands down my face.

Bryce's sweet, caregiving personality was going to drive me insane in the best possible way. I just fucking knew it.

Sunlight filtering through the curtains woke me up, and I groaned, flopping my arm over my eyes once I rolled to my back. The sun was pretty high in the sky, so I was guessing it somewhere around nine or ten in the morning.

Sighing, I sat up and padded out of my room and down the stairs, wanting some coffee. I hadn't had decent coffee in six years, and I was hoping Bryce had some and wasn't on some weird no-coffee diet due to football season approaching soon.

I stopped at the entrance to the kitchen when I saw Bryce sitting at the bar with an older woman next to him, both of them eating cookies. I snorted. "Cookies for breakfast?" I asked.

Bryce lifted his coffee mug with a smirk. "I at least have coffee to go with it." He set his coffee down and threw a thumb over his shoulder. "Coffee pot is by the stove. Coffee mugs are in the cabinet right above it. I've got flavored liquid creamers in the fridge."

"Thanks," I gruffly responded, wondering if the woman next to him was the woman he'd mentioned last night. Ms. Thomson, wasn't it?

I held my hand out to her before going to the coffee pot, determined to make a good impression on Bryce's friends. "I'm Pistol Cage," I introduced myself to her.

She beamed at me and then winked at Bryce as she shook my hand. "Ooh, a boy that's good-looking *and* has good manners," she teased. I chuckled. "I'm Beverly Thomson. It's nice to finally meet you, Pistol."

I released her hand and walked over to the coffee pot, listening as she began to tease Bryce. I could place money on it he was probably red as a tomato. He'd always had a bad habit of blushing.

"You're telling me you never tried to tap that?" Ms. Thomson asked Bryce, not even caring that I could hear her.

Bryce groaned. "Please don't ever say *tap that* again," he begged her. I barked out a laugh and added a spoonful of sugar to my coffee before stirring it and inhaling the sweet, black liquid. It smelled like heaven in a cup.

Bryce stood up and walked his mug

over to the sink, rinsing it out before sticking it in the dishwasher. Then, he grabbed his wallet out of his pocket and handed me a black credit card. I frowned, not reaching forward to take it. "Pistol, just take it please. You need clothes, at the very least."

"Bryce—"

He grabbed my hand and placed the card in it, and I was too distracted by the tingles that raced up my arm from where he was touching me to care that he was forcing me to take the card. He curled my fingers around it and then placed my hand back at my side. "Use the laptop in my office to order you some clothes. And have them rush shipped so they get here no later than tomorrow. I'll pick you up some clothes on my way back home from practice."

I didn't know what to say, so I said nothing at all. But Bryce always understood, and he offered me a small smile, his shoulders relaxing when he saw I wasn't going to protest any longer. "I'll be back this afternoon," he assured me. Then, he dropped a kiss to Ms. Thomson's cheek and disappeared out the front door.

Leaving me alone with her. Wasn't sure how I felt about that.

She shook her head and hummed. "That boy has it bad."

I frowned at her. "What does he have bad?"

She snorted and patted the seat beside her. "You're just as clueless as him, hun. Come on. Take a seat and eat some cookies with me."

I grunted but did as she instructed. Biting into one of the cookies, I groaned. "I'm never letting you leave," I mumbled. These were fucking *delicious*.

She laughed. "Bryce says that just about every day when I bring him these."

I side-eyed her. "Does his coach not care what he eats?"

She winked at me. "What his coach doesn't know won't hurt him."

I snickered. I liked her already.

I pulled the casserole out of the oven, my stomach rumbling at the scent. I'd made a chicken and rice casserole, and it looked *perfect*. Thankfully, I still had my touch with cooking, and the recipe I'd found in a healthy recipe book Bryce had laying around was easy to follow.

What hadn't been easy was finding ingredients to cook anything. He really needed to do some damn grocery shopping.

The front door opened, and a moment later, I heard keys hit the small table in the entrance before Bryce appeared in the kitchen. "I followed the smell of food," he said, grinning at me. "You cooked?"

I nodded. "Hope you like chicken and rice casserole. It's the only thing you had all the ingredients for."

He grimaced. "Yeah—I need to go grocery shopping."

I snorted. "No shit." I grabbed a plate from the cabinet and spooned him out a generous helping of food before passing it to him. He grabbed a fork from the drawer and stood at the counter to eat, not even bothering to sit down. Fuck, he must have been hungry.

"Coach is working us extra hard since the first game is coming up soon," he said, giving me an explanation for why he was so hungry. Guess we hadn't completely lost that intuitive thing between us in all these years, and I hated that I liked that so much. I was still head over heels in love with a guy that would never be able to love me. I wasn't even sure if Bryce was gay. I actually wasn't sure what his sexuality was at all. I mean, I'd never seen him with a guy or a woman.

The doorbell rang, and Bryce left his plate on the counter, heading to the door. A moment later as I was sitting with my food at the bar, he came in with a small box. He slid it to me. "I put you on my phone plan. I don't like not being able to get in touch with you."

I slowly pulled it toward me, trying not to wonder how much he just spent on this. It was the newest phone out—I knew that much from commercials on a TV show I watched today.

"Bryce—"

"Don't," he warned me. "You need a phone. Set it up when you get done eating."

I huffed. "It's expensive."

He shrugged at me before chewing his last bite of food. "And it's my money, so I get to decide what I want to spend it on." He rinsed his plate and fork before sticking them in the dishwasher. "I'm going to grab a shower and probably a nap. I'm fucking wiped. Get that set up, yeah?" He turned to look at me over his shoulder with a warm smile. My chest ached with longing for him. "And thanks for cooking dinner. It was really fucking good."

With that, he slipped from the kitchen, leaving me reeling and hopelessly fucking in love with him.

The house was silent, not even a TV on. I was pretty used to the silence, but with Bryce only down the hall from me, it made me yearn for him more.

I was hard—so fucking hard. I kept

picturing him in the shower, water running down his tight, lean body, his cock hanging heavy between his legs.

Fuuuck.

I gripped my cock in my fist, using my precum to lubricate my hand since I didn't have lotion. And like fuck was I looking through Bryce's house to find something to use. That would just bring about questions I wasn't ready to answer.

I groaned as I tightened my hand around myself, spreading my legs the slightest bit before I began to pump my fist, images of Bryce flashing through my mind. Would he let me touch him? Suck him to the back of my throat? Fuck, would he let me in that tight ass of his?

I swallowed a moan, pumping faster. I heard the door creak, and I pumped faster, watching through slitted eyes as Bryce ducked back out of view. *Fuck. Fuck.*

He was *watching* me. Did that mean he wanted me just as badly?

"I know you're there," I rasped, my hips raising off the bed.

The door slowly inched open, and then

Bryce appeared, his eyes running over my naked body before focusing on my hand around my cock. I slowed my pace, letting him see me. Licking my lips, I beckoned him closer, hoping I wasn't making a mistake. Bryce was all I had in this world, but my need for him was winning out over my common sense.

"Fuck, Pistol," he rasped, stepping closer. He was only wearing a pair of boxers, but they were tented, the front of them damp with precum. He sucked in a shuddered breath of air. His fingers twitched before he curled them into fists. "You want this, too?"

"*God, yes*," I groaned. "Drop those," I said, pointing at his boxers with my free hand, "and get your fine ass up here with me."

He quickly stripped out of his boxers before crawling onto the bed beside me. I released my cock and moved fast, spreading his thighs to expose his rim to my eyes. I ran my finger over that tight hole, and he twitched, a moan falling from his lips. "You ever been touched here?" He shook his head. "You ever been fucked before, Bryce?"

Swallowing thickly, his eyes shut, he shook his head again.

Fuuuck.

Yes. Yes. Yes. He was a virgin and all fucking mine.

I gripped his cock, giving it some leisurely strokes, loving the way his lips parted and he breathlessly whispered my name. "You want me to fuck you tonight, Bryce? Because I will, baby. I just need lube."

He panted, slowly opening his eyes to look at me. "My bathroom. Top drawer."

I quickly got off the bed and left my room, going to his. I didn't even take the time to take in details of his room. I was afraid if I took too long, he'd change his mind. So, I quickly grabbed the lube from where he said it was and headed back to my room, already popping the lid open and slicking up my fingers when I reentered.

He was slowly stroking his cock, and he

groaned as he ran his eyes over me, squeezing himself. “P-Pistol...” he moaned.

I moved back onto the bed and gently began to probe him open. He tensed at first, but then I sucked his cock into the back of my throat, knocking his hand away, and he loosened up for me, moaning so fucking loud, it was worthy of a porn star.

I sucked him hard but slow, taking my time to stretch him. I wasn’t small, and I wanted to make sure he was stretched enough to comfortably take me.

Just as he was about to come, I released him from my mouth. A sexy little whine fell from his lips, but then I pulled my fingers out of him and slicked up my cock. “I’m clean,” I told him. “Haven’t fucked anyone since college, and I was tested a couple of weeks before I landed my ass in prison.”

“Bare,” he begged, the only word he was able to utter.

I pressed the tip of my cock to that tight ring of muscle. He tensed, but I gripped his cock and began to stroke him. “Relax for me, baby,” I soothed. “It’s going to burn at first, but I promise I’ll make it feel good.”

He blew out a soft breath and then forced his body to relax. "There you go. Now bear down for me."

With gritted teeth, he bore down, and I began to slide inside of him. I moaned, my head falling back for a moment. He was so fucking *tight* and warm. *Fuck.*

I forced my head back down to watch him. His lips were parted, and he moaned my name when I bumped his prostate, his cock jerking. Oh, he wouldn't last long, but I planned to fuck him until we were both too exhausted to go any longer.

I bottomed out, groaning his name, my chest heaving. He reached for me, and I complied, moving my body over his, hooking the back of his knees over my arms before I began to pump in and out of him, my lips meeting his in a hard, bruising kiss.

"You're *mine*," I growled.

He nodded, clinging to me, kissing me with desperation. "Love you," he panted. "Loved you for years, Pistol."

He came then, his seed spilling between us, and I fucked him harder, letting him know without words how fucking much he meant to me. And only when I was about to come did I whisper those words to him, too.

He came with me, his ass milking my cock for everything I could give him.

Chapter Six

Bryce

PATRIOT'S QUARTERBACK SHACKING UP WITH CRIMINAL

F*uck.*

This couldn't goddamn be happening. Not already. Shit, he'd barely been out a damn week. We'd barely even been together. Someone must have seen us out last week when we went grocery shopping, and yeah, we'd been holding hands because I had nothing to hide.

And I must have gotten a fucking tail

on the way home. No doubt they'd been camped out somewhere, and I hadn't noticed.

Shit.

How in the hell was Pistol going to take this? He had enough to deal with without being in the spotlight, too. Christ, I had a feeling this might happen, but I was hoping he would be more on his feet first, more grounded and sure of what he was going to do.

"I don't like that look on your face," Pistol said, wrapping his arms around my waist and resting his chin on my shoulder. "Well, shit," he muttered, reading my phone over my shoulder.

Gritting my teeth, I began to read the article, knowing Pistol was reading it as well over my shoulder. Might as well get all the facts in line so I knew how to address this when I was confronted about it. And no doubt, I *would* face questions. I had my first game in a week. Reporters were the fucking sharks of the sports world, and they would chew me up and spit me the fuck out if I didn't find out what everyone was saying.

> *Patriot's quarterback, Bryce Cutler, was seen three nights ago holding hands with a man no one has ever seen before. It has left us all reeling and confused, wondering if the very eligible bachelor has been claimed—by a man, no less.*

Fucking trashy ass articles. I goddamn hated them.

> *Turns out, the two of them live together, and after doing some digging, the identity of the unknown man was identified.*

> *Pistol Cage. And it seems he's just been granted parole and is serving out the rest of his sentence in Bryce Cutler's house.*

I set the phone down, not wanting to read anymore. "I hate those trashy articles," I grumbled, reaching up to rub my forehead.

"Hey," Pistol said quietly, turning me to face him. My eyes met his, and he crookedly smiled at me, settling my nerves. "We'll figure this out, you hear me? I don't give a fuck what they have to say about me. I stopped caring about what people thought a long time ago, baby." He gripped the back of my neck and pulled my lips to his, kissing me so thoroughly that I even forgot my own damn name.

I rested my forehead on his shoulder, sinking into his embrace when he wrapped his arms back around me, rubbing my back. "I need to call my agent," I murmured, resting my hands on his hips. "Think you can whip us up some breakfast?" I asked, looking up at him.

He kissed me again. "Go do what you need to do. I'll get breakfast and coffee going," he assured me.

I slipped from the kitchen and headed into my office, my phone already pulled up to my ear. Jace answered on the second ring. "Please tell me you're not shacking up with a convict," Jace pleaded when he answered, not even bothering with a hello.

"Who I decide to *shack up* with is none of your fucking concern. And to save your job, refrain from calling him a fucking convict, yeah?"

He grunted. Jace was a damn good agent, but he could be a rotten asshole, too. But he also knew I was the best damn player he had, and if he lost me, he lost a shit ton of money.

And if there was one thing Jace was, he was fucking money-greedy.

"Pistol is an old friend of mine, who is now my boyfriend," I began to explain. I tapped my fingertips on the desk to help keep me calm and focused. "He had it pretty fucking rough growing up, and he had his shit together in college."

"Reports are saying he got kicked out."

"He did," I said, not bothering to lie. That wasn't who I was. I faced shit head-on. "He had to stay with his dad during break. He says he didn't smoke, and I believe him. But apparently, his dad puts pot in everything, and Pistol believes he ate something with weed in it."

"Christ," Jace muttered.

I blew out a soft breath. "He got kicked off the football team, and shortly after, he got kicked out of school. From what I understand, he lived in his truck for a couple of weeks, trying to find a job to get on his feet, but he was broke as fuck and still sitting at zero, so when his dad called and offered for him to take a job, he took it."

"And it landed his ass in jail," Jace put together.

"Yeah." I scrubbed my hand down my face. "He served six years and finally reached out to me. I had no idea he was locked up. When I couldn't locate him, I figured he wanted me to stay away, so I did. He's been clean and has stayed out of trouble his entire time in prison. Even the judge commended him on that. He's here to stay the hell out of trouble and away from his family. And I'm going to help him get on his feet."

"And you don't think being his boyfriend might complicate that?" Jace asked in all seriousness.

"No." I didn't believe that. Because since Pistol had been here, he'd been applying for jobs and trying to figure things out for himself, even if he hadn't had any luck yet. Just a bunch of rejection letters. "He's trying, Jace. And I'm not fucking abandoning him, no matter what it might do to my career. He needs someone in his corner, and I love him."

A throat cleared from the door of my office. I jerked my eyes. Pistol was standing in my doorway with eggs, bacon, toast, and coffee, his eyes a little wide as he stared at me.

"Shit," I whispered, standing up. "Jace, hold on a minute." I put the phone on mute and set it down before taking the mug and plate from him, setting it on my desk as well. "How much did you hear?"

"Just the um... the last part," he said, clearing his throat. He ran his eyes over me. "Did you mean that, Bryce?"

Swallowing thickly, I nodded. We'd set it weeks ago in the heat of the moment our first time together, but neither of us had brought it up since. Did he think I'd been lying?

God, I would never lie to him.

"I love you, Pistol. Been in love with you for fucking years, and I'm *not* letting you go, even if it might cost me my career."

He looked like he'd been shoved on his

ass, the wind knocked out of his lungs. He cleared his throat and shoved his hand through his hair, almost as if he didn't know what to do with himself.

"I'm not a good man," he finally rasped, looking at me, his eyes sad.

I stepped closer to him and gripped his sides, drawing him to me. "Your past does not define you, Pistol. The man you are now—*that* is what defines you. Not a goddamn thing else, you hear me? I love you. And I don't need to hear those words from you. But I need you to know that."

He gripped the side of my neck and kissed me, prying my lips apart before he deepened it. I groaned into his mouth, plastering my body to his larger, more muscular one, unable to get enough of him or get close enough.

"I'll do my best to make you not regret it," Pistol rasped, resting his forehead on mine.

I pressed a kiss to the tip of his nose. "You could never make me regret loving you, Pistol," I told him honestly.

* * *

Pistol was sitting on the floor of the living room, my laptop open in front of him as he scoured entry-level job positions that he hadn't yet applied for. I sat behind him on the couch, my legs on either side of him. He groaned when I began to gently massage his shoulders. He was tense as hell. Probably needed to take him with me when I went to my next massage appointment. It was clear he needed one.

"My agent has a plan, but I need you to agree to it before I text him confirmation."

Pistol grunted. "I'm listening."

"He wants me to do an interview this weekend after my game, and he wants you there with me. Show the world we're a unit and nothing they say will break us apart. And he thinks it'll do some good to show people that being arrested and serving time isn't the end of the world, that you can pick up your pieces and create a better future."

He sighed. "I fucking hate being the center of attention." I pressed a kiss to the top of his head. “But I’ll do it. Just let me know all the details.”

“Jace will probably reach out to you,” I warned him as I fished my phone from my pocket, “so don’t freak out if he does. He’s probably just going to run over everything with you. And if he starts grilling you or makes you uncomfortable, don’t be afraid to put him in his place. He knows who signs his checks.”

Pistol snorted. “I kind of like the over-protective side of you,” he said, turning around to face me. He slid his hands up my thighs and then began to unfasten my jeans. I groaned, dropping my head back on the couch.

As soon as my shaft was freed, he sucked me to the back of his throat. And *fuuuck*, Pistol could suck dick.

I laced my fingers in his short hair, gripping the strands. “Fuck yes,” I moaned, watching him through slitted eyes. I sucked in a sharp breath of air when he swallowed around me. “*Christ*,” I swore. “You look so fucking good with my dick in your mouth, Pistol,” I groaned.

He sucked harder, swirling his tongue around my tip, swallowing around me when he sucked me deep. In no time at all, I was shooting my cum down the back of his throat, roaring his name.

I was pretty sure he took the soul straight out of my body.

Chapter Seven

Bryce

Coach was fucking brutal today, and I had a feeling it had everything to do with my name being smeared through the fucking headlines faster than a rattlesnake could strike its victim.

I guzzled a bottle of water like I was dying of dehydration. The team was oddly quiet today. They all knew I was gay, so that was no shocker for them. I'd told them all I was gay the moment I was brought into that locker room for the very first time, and they'd had no qualms about it.

I was pretty sure they were wary of the fact that the guy they looked up to, the guy that never had his face in the tabloids, the guy that had never been gossiped about before, was now rumored to be shacking up with a criminal on parole.

"Bro, are the tabloids true?" Henley finally asked me, obviously the first on the team to get up the guts to pry into my private life. They knew how close to the heart I kept my shit, even though I was friendly with all of them.

"Mostly," I told him, nodding my head. I swiped my hand over my sweaty face, grimacing. Damn, I needed a shower, but I wasn't sure if Coach was done with us yet. "It's a long story, but he's a good guy. I would never do anything to jeopardize my career unless it was for a good reason, and all of you know that."

Kelly, who'd obviously been listening in, clapped his hand to my shoulder pad. "We know, brother, and we trust you. Just nice to have it clarified."

I nodded in understanding. Coach

stormed over, pointing his finger at me. I swallowed my anxiety. "Cutler, my fucking office. *Now*!" he barked, turning on his heel and storming off. "Rest of you, get fucking showers. You reek."

I blew out a soft breath and followed Coach down the field to the entrance of the locker rooms. We bypassed them, heading further up the hall where his office was located. As soon as I walked inside, he slammed the door shut behind me.

"Do you know the shit show you've caused?" he asked me. "Whole integrity of the team is being questioned now, wondering if we support criminals who traffic drugs—the same drugs that rip families apart when someone gets addicted."

I clenched my jaw, trying not to fly off the handle. I didn't like what he was implying. While I knew what drugs were capable of doing, had seen what they did to Pistol firsthand, I didn't like Pistol being thrown into that bunch.

"Coach, he's a decent guy. He's one of the best guys I know."

He twirled his finger around his ear. "Is your judgment fucking screwy, Cutler? Did you endure a head injury during the off-season? He trafficked drugs, Cutler. Point, blank, period. The fuck do you have to say for yourself?"

I clenched my jaw, working it around to calm myself. Finally forcing it to relax before I started grinding my teeth, I looked back at one of the men I respected most in this world. I knew he was just looking out for the team, and I understood that. But he was coming at me sideways without knowing everything.

"Pistol—"

"What a goddamn name," Coach muttered.

I loudly cleared my throat. The look he shot me could've frozen Hell, but I stood my ground. "Pistol," I began again, "grew up in a shit hole of a home. His father was abusive, sold drugs, did drugs, and drank himself sick day in and day out." Coach remained quiet, hearing me out. "He got a football scholarship to college, which is how we met. Not once have I ever seen him high or drunk. He studied the best he could, though school wasn't his strong suit. He was standoffish, an asshole, and as rude and blunt as they come, but he and I got along. I'm pretty sure I was the closest thing he had to a friend."

I shoved my hand through my sweaty hair, my other hand tightening around my helmet. "I didn't know Pistol didn't have anywhere to go during Thanksgiving break, and if you decided to stay on campus, you had to pay." Coach grunted, obviously not liking that bit. "So, Pistol went home. He swears he didn't get high, and Coach, I believe him. He was staying in a home with a father who liked to eat edibles as much as he liked to smoke. We were all randomly drug tested when we came back from Thanksgiving break, and Pistol failed the drug test."

Coach stayed quiet, so I continued. "He was kicked off the football team, and not long after, he got kicked out of school, too. He lived in his truck for two weeks, applying for jobs with no luck, and when his dad called wanting him to do a run, something he hadn't done since high school, he took it because he needed the money if he wanted food to eat."

"And he got caught," Coach easily put together. I nodded. Coach shook his head and dropped into his chair. "*Shit.* Why can't shit ever be clean-cut? Why do kids have to go through so much goddamn bull-shit, never getting the real opportunity to break the fucking cycle because the world makes it so damn hard to do so?"

I shrugged. If I knew that answer, I'd have started fixing shit for Pistol the moment I knew he was locked up. But I didn't have the answers, so I was out here doing the best I could.

Starting with not giving up on him like everyone else had in his life.

"Coach, I'm not giving up on him. I promised him I never would, and I'm not breaking that promise. He's had way too many people walk out as it is. So, do what you need to do, and let me know what the outcome is."

He held up his hand. "Wait." He pinched the bridge of his nose before blowing out a soft breath. "Has your agent been in touch with you?"

I nodded. "Yeah. He's scheduling an interview for Monday night after our game."

Coach nodded, drumming his fingers on the desk. "Do the interview. Continue living as you are, and don't go into hiding. I'll work with the press department and figure out a good way to spin this." He looked up at me. "It shows integrity and a hell of a lot of loyalty that you're willing to stand by his side despite all the shit pouring into the media about the two of you right now."

I shrugged. "I've never cared much about what people have to say, Coach, and I'm learning to care even less with Pistol by my side. I think the world could learn a lot from a man like him, if I'm being honest."

Coach hummed. "Go get showered and changed, Cutler. And rest up. I'm working you guys even harder tomorrow."

I bit back my groan as I left his office. But when I announced to the guys what to expect tomorrow, Coach shouted for everyone to stop making dying walrus sounds.

Pistol

I looked up when the sound of Bryce's keys hitting the table in the foyer reached my ears. He dragged himself into the kitchen, looking tired and worn out. I frowned.

"Everything okay?"

He nodded, dropping onto one of the stools at the bar. "Hungry. Tired. Coach is kicking our asses this week."

I grimaced. "I miss playing football until I remember how brutal practices can be."

Bryce cracked a smile at that. I put a sandwich in front of him with a protein shake. "I turned on the pool heater this morning. Thought a swim might be good to help loosen your muscles after practice. Guess it's a good thing I thought ahead."

He glanced up at me from beneath his lashes. "You planning on joining me, baby?"

I pushed his wet hair back from his face, hating how exhausted he looked. And I had a feeling it would only get worse at the season wore on. "I'll join you anywhere," I assured him. "Eat that. I'll go grab your swim shorts and a towel."

"Thanks, babe."

I slipped out of the kitchen and into his room, grabbing a pair of black swim shorts and his matching black beach towel, taking them into the kitchen so he didn't have to walk a mile to get dressed and then go back to the pool. He pulled me in for a quick kiss before I left the kitchen again, this time heading to my room to change.

Wasn't even sure if this was still my room anymore, to be honest. Bryce never let me sleep without him. But then again, when he was away for games, I would want my own bed to sleep in. Especially since I couldn't follow him all over the country. If I did, I'd be violating the fuck out of my probation.

I wasn't keen on landing my ass right back in prison. That was a hell-no and no-thank-you from me.

After changing into a matching pair of black shorts and grabbing a matching black towel, I headed into the kitchen, my cock jumping in my shorts at the sight of Bryce. He had stripped out of his clothes, leaving them on the floor where they landed, and was standing in front of me in just his black shorts, his tight, lean body on full display for me to ogle.

I had no idea how I was so fucking lucky to be able to call him mine, but I'd *never* take it for granted.

"Fuck, you look good enough to eat," I groaned.

Bryce reached out, and I stepped closer, placing my hand on his hip, pulling him to me. He wrapped his arms around me, angling his head for a soft, deep, tender kiss. I groaned into his mouth, tugging him tighter against me. Leaning back against the counter, I spread my legs, pulling him between them. His hard shaft pressed against mine, but I didn't grind us together. I just continued to languidly kiss him, enjoying this moment between us.

"I love you," Bryce murmured when I

parted our lips the slightest bit so we could catch our breaths.

"I love you," I rasped. I'd never get tired of hearing those words from him, and even more, I'd never get sick of telling him I loved him, too. This man had saved my life. I was head over heels for him, and if I lost him, I wouldn't care what happened to me. My life would be over. Done. My will to live gone right along with him.

"Let's get in the pool," Bryce said, but he ran his hands down my sides, like he wasn't ready to let me go yet. Fuck, I couldn't blame him. I wasn't ready to let him go either, but he needed the water on his muscles. And his needs would always come before my wants.

"Pool," I told him. "After, we can fuck all you want."

He groaned, lust darkening his eyes. "Promise?" he growled, grinding our cocks together.

"*Fuck,*" I hissed, gently pushing him back from me. "Pool, Bryce."

He barked out a laugh and walked away, heading toward the sliding glass door.

"I'm holding you to that promise of a fuck later," he tossed over his shoulder.

I snorted. I had no fucking doubt about that in my mind. And now, my dick was *never* going to soften until it sank deep inside his ass.

Chapter Eight

Pistol

I was nervous as fuck for this interview. Like, sick to my stomach, I-want-to-vomit-everywhere kind of nervous.

This wasn't who I was. I didn't normally get nervous over anything anymore unless it concerned Bryce's reaction to something. I'd even faced that judge in the courtroom without an ounce of fear or nerves. I was prepared to be thrown right back into prison, my parole denied.

But this was different. I knew how important this was to Bryce, how important this was for his career, for his team. And I didn't want to fuck up things for him. His teammates looked up to him to make the right choices, and he'd told me they stood behind him on this, but still.

Our story—*my* story—could destroy all of their faith in their captain. My past could get Bryce kicked off the team, his pro career destroyed. And while he'd told me over and over that he had way more money than he knew what to do with and he would always live comfortably, I knew money wouldn't be the root of the issue.

Bryce lived and breathed football, and he was *excellent* at it. I didn't want him to lose that dream because he'd decided to stick by my side and keep his promise to me. It meant the world to me that he was so determined, but I also feared for him, for his future.

"You ready?" Jace, Bryce's agent, asked as he stepped up beside me. He straightened his suit. No doubt it was stupidly expensive. I didn't care how much money I might make one day, I'd never spend a godawful amount on clothes.

And I was glad to see that despite the money Bryce was swimming in, he was still just as down-to-Earth as he had been in college. Hell, looking at his house, the regular sedan he drove, and the clothes he wore, you'd never guess Bryce had a lot of money. He took living within his means to a whole other level.

I blew out a soft breath and pulled at the collar of my t-shirt. It wasn't constricting, but right then, my entire body felt squeezed into too small clothes.

"Ready as I'll ever be," I grunted.

Which was not ready at all.

I watched as Bryce took his seat behind the mic. They won the game by a landslide, though Bryce always made sure they never ran the score up to an insane number out of respect for the other team. It was another reason so many sports followers respected him, even if they hated his team. He wasn't out here for the clout. He was truly out there, playing his heart out solely for his love of the game.

Bryce cleared his throat when reporters began throwing questions at him left and right. I had no idea how he kept up with all of it. All of their words were just sort of thrown together, sounding jumbled to my own ears.

"If you'll give me a moment, I'll answer each question individually and in an organized manner," Bryce said. Slowly, the reporters began to get quieter until they were silent altogether. Bryce looked over at me, a small smile tilting his lips. "Babe, will you join me?"

Whispers sounded throughout the crowd. With my chin tilted up the slightest bit, I made my way onto the small stage and took my seat beside Bryce. He grabbed my hand in his and then leaned over, gripped my chin, and pressed his lips to mine.

Flashes from cameras assaulted my vision, and I winced. I had no idea how he continuously put up with this week in and week out. It would drive me nuts.

"First, I want to introduce my boyfriend to you all," Bryce began, looking out into the crowd. But he never released my hand. I gave his a gentle squeeze to let him know I was thankful for it. Not much got under my skin, but this stupid interview was.

The things I did for this man, I swear.

He cast me a small smile before aiming his focus back at the crowd of reporters in front of us. I noticed his teammates were standing in the back, no doubt there to support him through this interrogation. Because that's what this felt like. A fucking interrogation.

"This is Pistol Cage. That's his name. Not convict. Not criminal. Not druggie. Not gay man. *Pistol Cage*," he repeated with more emphasis. My heart flipped in my chest. "I've known Pistol since his freshman year of college when he showed up on the football field looking like he'd seen better days. He had dark circles under his eyes, he was badly in need of a haircut, and it was clear his clothes were just about one wash away from completely falling apart."

I clenched my jaw when I saw one woman whisper something to the man next to her, both of them side-eyeing me.

"But despite what he looked like, I still

held out my hand and introduced myself to him. He was rude. Blunt. But you know what else he was? A hard worker. He didn't give up. He fought for what he wanted. And *that* I could respect, just as everyone here should respect it, too."

He glanced over at me. "I won't tell his story. It's up to him when he takes the floor to tell you anything. But I beg of you, please have an open mind. Don't judge him for the mistakes he's made."

I cleared my throat, taking my cue. "I know many of you here have already made up your mind about me," I gruffly began, my voice rougher and a bit deeper than Bryce's. Instantly, all eyes turned to me, the microphones held a little closer, no doubt so my voice came through clearer. "I won't fool you into thinking I care about what you publish about me because I don't. The only thing I care about in those articles is Bryce and his reputation because he's done nothing wrong here."

One of his teammates cheered and fist-pumped the air, and I grinned, unable to help myself. I shook my head, huskily laughing. Bryce tightened his hand around mine, his thumb rubbing against my skin. "I won't go into sordid details. My father was a drunk, and he was high more than he was ever sober. Life was hell when I was growing up, but I made it. And Thanksgiving week during my sophomore year, I couldn't afford to stay on campus, so I went home. I'm guessing I ended up eating an edible; weed was in everything in that house, but I did my best to be careful. Got drug tested when I came back and failed it. It killed my football career, and a couple of days later, my college career followed when I was kicked out of school."

I cleared my throat, hating that I couldn't lean back in my chair. I never wanted to sit through another one of these interviews again.

"What landed me in jail was poor choices on my part. I'd been living in my truck for two weeks, I was down to my last few dollars. I needed money, and I needed it faster than any of the businesses I'd applied to were calling me back, which was none." I blew out a soft breath. "So, when my dad called, I answered." Then, I grinned. "And I just outed him on public TV," I said with a snort. I shook my head, laughing softly, unable to believe myself. But at least he'd finally get the karma he deserved.

There was no way law enforcement officials would ignore this—not when it was airing on national television.

Dad would be pissed, but oh well. He'd shoved me aside as soon as I was no longer useful to him, and he'd cost me six years of my life, leaving me thinking I had no other choice but to do his bidding.

So, fuck him.

"I reached out to Bryce a few weeks ago. I never expected a response, but not only did he write back, but he immediately began moving mountains to make it possible for me to live with him, where I would have a fresh start." I looked over at him, emotion clogging my throat for a moment, preventing me from speaking. Once I was able to dislodge it, I rasped, "I love him for everything he's done for me. I love him for the man he's always been. He's selfless and kind and everything good in this world."

Bryce gripped the back of my neck and crushed our mouths together. Cheers rang out throughout the room, but I didn't care.

We were announcing on public television that we were in this together, and nothing—not the media or the fans—would rip us apart.

"Should we expect to see more of you together then?" one of the reporters asked once we broke apart, our chests heaving. My cock was rock hard in my jeans. I'd been over this interview before it even started, but now, I was on the verge of walking out just so I could fuck Bryce and claim his ass as mine all over again.

Bryce chuckled, his cheeks flushed, that gorgeous blush on his cheeks. "Yeah, definitely." He winked at me. "Pistol isn't going anywhere. He's here to stay."

His teammates cheered for him again—even louder this time. And unable to help myself, I cupped Bryce's cheek and pulled his lips back to mine again.

He was all fucking mine.

Epilogue

Pistol

A LITTLE OVER A YEAR LATER

I wiped the sleeve of my long-sleeve orange shirt across my forehead, wiping some of the sweat away so it wouldn't drip so badly into my eyes. I was wearing a ball cap, but that didn't stop my sweat from running down my face like someone had turned a water hose on me.

It'd been a little over a year since I'd gotten out of prison. I was still on parole, but there was talk of it shortening. The judge, I guessed, was pretty fucking impressed by what I'd done so far to change my life around.

I was the proud owner of a lawn care business. I started out in Bryce's neighborhood—well, guessed it was mine now, too since we lived together still—cutting yards for Mrs. Thomson and Mr. Ingle, who lived across the street from us. Then, Mr. Johnson, who Bryce normally helped rake leaves when he had time, called on me to help him, and before I knew it, I was tending his yard, too.

Word eventually spread to Mrs. Orson, and before long, my name was spreading like wildfire throughout the neighborhood. It didn't take long for the business cards Bryce created and had printed were being handed out all over the city, people calling me left and right. I got so busy, I had to hire two more crews.

Bryce forced me to hire an assistant. They worked from home for me, tending to my appointments, letting me know of sudden changes, and other shit I didn't really give a damn about doing myself, which left me to do the hard work that I loved doing.

But I knew that none of this would have been possible without Bryce. After three months of trying and failing to get hired somewhere—even McDonald's wouldn't hire me—I knew I had to do something else. But what, I didn't know. And when I mentioned to Bryce at dinner one night that I needed to figure something else out, he tried to give me money to help start this business.

I turned him down flat, but eventually, he got me to cave enough to at least take it as a loan—with interest. I refused to only pay him back what he'd loaned me.

Boy, he had been *pissed* about it though. But that was alright; I fucked the grumpiness out of him later that night.

A grin tilted my lips. My man was such a slut for cock.

I glanced at my dirty watch, grunting when I couldn't even read the screen. I swiped it on my black cargo pants and then pulled it back up to my face, looking at the time.

Bryce would be getting home soon—finally. Yesterday was his last game of the season—the Superbowl—and the Patriots won. Barely, but they fucking won. It had been a good game, and for a while, I'd been screaming at the TV and my husband.

Husband. God, I fucking loved calling him that.

Shortly after our interview, we got married. And still, a year after that interview, we were a sort of *it couple*. Did Bryce get backlash for being openly gay? Yeah, he did. A lot of people thought he shouldn't even be allowed to play football if he was gay. But his teammates didn't care, his hardcore fans didn't care, and his coach sure as fuck didn't.

So their opinions didn't matter. My man would continue doing what he loved—playing ball. And while they might have him ninety percent of the time during the season, I had him the rest of the year, and I couldn't fucking wait to finally come home to him every damn night again.

"Alright, boys, start wrapping this up!" I called out to my crew. They knew we were clocking off early today, and since we were working Mrs. Olson's yard today, she was perfectly okay with me splitting her yard between two days since she knew Bryce was coming home.

Sometimes, I felt like our neighborhood was more obsessed with our love life than we were, but in a weird way, I loved it. I loved the sense of community. I loved waking up every morning, finding Mrs. Thomson already sitting in one of the rockers on the front porch with a tray of freshly baked cookies.

It was a miracle I hadn't gained any weight considering my mornings always started off with coffee and cookies. Eggs? Pancakes? Bacon? Sausage? Who the fuck needed that when you had cookies in front of you?

I began helping load up equipment, and once everything was loaded, I drove my crew back to the yard so they could get in their personal vehicles and go home.

I'd started off with our house as my base for working, but within three months of me opening the business, I rented a warehouse with garage doors where all my work trucks and trailers easily fit. I'd been lucky to find the property, and when I'd grabbed it, it had only been on the rental market for two days. The parking lot beside the building was big enough to hold all of my employees' vehicles and then some, which was extremely helpful.

"Your man is coming home today, ain't he?" one of the younger guys, Falcon, asked me. He was a shorter guy and built stocky. I'd hired him straight out of juvie. His parents didn't let him come back home, and he'd been walking down the sidewalk, trying to find a job when he'd spotted me. I'd hired him on the spot, trained him, and let him sleep in the warehouse until he got on his feet.

I nodded at him. "Yeah, finally. Missed him like fucking crazy."

He laughed. "If you want to go on home, I can wash off all the equipment," he told me. "And I can just shoot you the time I'm done."

I nodded at him. "Sounds good, kid. See

if any of the other guys want to help, and just let me know who stays."

He nodded. "Will do, Pistol."

I walked out of the warehouse and over to my truck. It didn't take me long to get home, and Bryce's car was already in the driveway when I pulled in. I'd been hoping to beat him home, but I guessed he was just as eager to see me as I was him.

I quietly stepped into the house, listening for a sign of him. The sound of the shower in our room reached my ears. After I toed off my boots by the front door, I headed up the stairs, grimacing at the grass that fell from me. I'd have to vacuum that up later.

After stripping out of my clothes in the bedroom, I quietly made my way into the bathroom. Bryce was standing under the water, his head tilted back, but he jerked in surprise, his eyes opening when I pulled the door open and stepped in with him.

The heated look he sent me could've brought me to my knees. And when he licked those fucking lips, I almost fell.

No words were needed. I backed him

up against the wall and lifted him, our mouths hungrily fusing together. He moaned, his tongue tangling with mine, his fingers plunging into my hair.

"You need a haircut," he rasped when I released his lips and began attacking the skin of his throat.

"Shut up," I growled, making him laugh. But that laugh was abruptly cut off when I grabbed the bottle of lube off the shelf and began to slick him up. He groaned, the sound deep and primal, his nails digging into my back, drawing blood.

"Fuck, Pistol," he rasped. Gripping my hair, he dragged my mouth back to his, shamelessly grinding on my fingers as I worked on stretching him. "Need you," he panted.

"You ready for me?" I asked him. I wanted inside him so badly I almost couldn't think past my need for him, but I'd never hurt him.

He nodded, his lips hungrily moving over my jaw and down my throat before he sank his teeth into my collarbone. Pain burst behind my eyelids, and with a growl, I slammed up into him, sinking all the way into his heat, shouting his name as I did so.

"Yes!" he shouted, his head thrown back as I began to fuck him, shamelessly screwing him against the tiled wall. I couldn't fucking get enough of him. "Fuck, Pistol—harder."

I cursed, pummeling into him. He was going to have trouble walking later, but like I gave a fuck. What my man wanted, he fucking got.

It didn't take long for him to come, spilling between us. I swiped it up, and with his dazed eyes locked on mine, I licked my fingers clean, wickedly grinning at him afterward.

"Fucking hell," he rasped, dragging my mouth back to his, tasting himself on my tongue.

"Welcome home, babe," I growled.

And then, I came inside of him, marking him as mine all over again.

Want a glimpse into their future?

https://dl.bookfunnel.com/hglxtz6uee

Stay In Contact!

Want to stay up-to-date with sales, new releases, new preorders, etc?

Join my newsletter!

https://westgreenebooks.com

Facebook

Instagram

Facebook Group

Mastadon

Twitter

Patreon

Pinterest

Access my merch store here.

About West Greene

West Greene is a romance author that specializes in short, steamy books and erotic shorts.

All your instalove needs can be found in one of her books, whether you're looking for possessive men, men with no morals, spicy FF romance, a boy just needing his Daddy, a twink just needing love, or even the other woman to get her HEA.

West Greene refuses to be stuck in one trope or type of romance. She loves variety, and she's definitely going to share that variety with her readers.

www.ingramcontent.com/pod-product-compliance
Ingram Content Group UK Ltd.
Pitfield, Milton Keynes, MK11 3LW, UK
UKHW041957190726
13854UKWH00005B/2024

9 798215 805374